# THE FANTASTIC WORLD OF THE
# Oddies®

For my FANTASTIC parents
Patricia and Deryk

Oddies Ltd, 1 Hay Hill, London, W1J 6DH
www.oddieworld.com

Text copyright © Oddies Ltd, 2004
Illustrations copyright © Oddies Ltd, 2004

The right of Grant Slatter and Alex Hallatt as the author and illustrator of the
Work have been asserted by them in accordance with the Copyright, Designs
and Patents Act 1988.

A CIP catalogue record for this book is available from the British Library.

First Published in Great Britain in 2004 by Oddies Ltd.

ISBN 1-904745-05-9

Printed in Great Britain

# THE STORY OF
# Rugby Oddie

By Grant Slatter and Alex Hallatt

The rugby player put his clothes and his favourite pair of rugby socks into the washing machine.

"Chug chug whirr, chug chug whirr," went the washing machine. Then it did something strange.

It speeded up really fast and there were sparkles and a tinkling sound then a little 'pop!' Something magical had happened and one of the socks had disappeared.

The missing sock was called Jonny and he was off to Oddieworld for an adventure!

"This is what I call an away game!" he said in his tough voice.

Jonny popped out of the sockhole and into Oddieworld.
"Hello," said a soft voice behind him.

It was Sock Fairy. "My naughty sister, Witchy, has made Good Oddie River stop flowing and we have no water," she said. Jonny turned to look at the river.

"How did Witchy do that?" he said. "And how
can I help? I dont know how to make
rivers start flowing again."

But Sock Fairy had disappeared, leaving a shiny new rugby ball in her place. Jonny picked up the ball and started walking along the river.

Soon he came to Magic Lake. Divey the Diver Oddie was stuck
in the mud in the middle. "Don't worry Divey," said Jonny,
"I am going to sort this out - you just stay right there."

"Stay right here?" said Divey. "I'm STUCK right here!"
"Oh yes, er, just keep calm then,"
said Jonny as he hurried on.

Around the next bend Jonny saw what was blocking the river a huge whale! "Oh no, not whales," he said. "They're always trouble, away from home!"

There were lots of different Oddies trying to move the whale
and Firey was busy keeping it happy with his hose.
"A Witchy Spell did this,"
he said sternly.

Wizzo appeared and cast a special Floaty Spell, but just ended up floating off himself!

"Listen everyone!" said Jonny loudly.
"We need to turn the whale so it can slide down the river
and we need to work as a team. So lets make a scrum!"

Jonny got everyone into position, then shouted "PUSH!"
But no one moved. He tried again, but still no one moved.
"Oh no," he groaned, "they can't hear me in the scrum!"

Then he thought of the present from Sock Fairy. He
quickly put the rugby ball into the scrum and everyone
saw it go in and pushed hard. The whale slowly turned.

As soon as it was facing down the river the whale started to move forward. "Come on everyone - let's have a ride," said Jonny.

The whale started to slide down the river, faster and faster.
They shot past Divey at Magic Lake...

...and into the sea with a huge SPLASH!

Sailor Oddie was passing and helped everyone back to Heel Beach.

Then they heard a familiar voice.
"Well done Jonny!"

It was Sock Fairy. "We'd love you to stay in Oddieworld forever,"
she said, "but I'll magic you back if you really want me to."
And what do you think Jonny did?

He chose to stay. "I think we make a great team," he said.
"Now who's for a rugby match?"

The rugby match was great fun. Jonny scored a try and won the game with a perfect drop kick in the last minute.

BOOF!

After the match both teams shook toes, then sang songs together and drank pints and pints of beer...ginger beer!

Back home the rugby player searched everywhere for his missing sock, but didn't find it.

Later, as he got into bed, he asked himself...

"Where do those missing Odd Socks go?"

# OTHER ODDIES BOOKS

This is the sixth book in the Oddies series. Others are available separately or as part of a gift pack. Visit our fantastic web site for more details - our web address is www.oddieworld.com

Oddies books can also be ordered through all good bookshops.

# THE FANTASTIC WORLD OF THE

## Oddies®

WWW.ODDIEWORLD.COM

# CUT OUT AND COLOUR IN

© Oddies Ltd. Find more games at www.oddieworld.com

# WWW.ODDIEWORLD.COM

Take a trip to Oddieworld and help your kids gain basic computer skills. Learn through play with the Oddies!

* Puzzle Games
* Colour-in Games
* Matching Games
* Competitions
* Send Free OddieCards

Complete the secret game on our web site and get a FREE oddies poster!
(a big one)

THE FANTASTIC WORLD OF THE

# Oddies®

WWW.ODDIEWORLD.COM

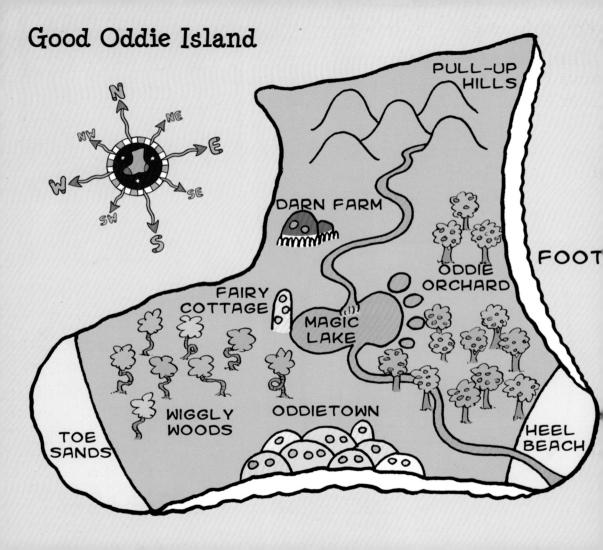